The Real Tooth Fairies®

A Real Fairytale now revealed to Earthies
By Royal Decree of Real Fairyland's Queen Sirona

Royal Council
of the
Official Seal
Love is Magic®

Real Fairyland®

Published by Royal Council of the Real Fairyland, LLC
On the seaside Acorn Trail leading to the ancient fairy portal of Airlie
Wilmington, North Carolina

www.TheRealToothFairies.com

First Edition, September 2009   Printed in China
Library of Congress Cataloging-in-Publication Data
Frankel, Rachel E.
Stacey Becomes a Real Tooth Fairy, Book 2/ by Rachel E. Frankel; illustrated by A-M Basom & Kelly Grupczynski.
--1st ed.   p. cm -- (The Real Tooth Fairies series)
Summary: On her nightly trip to Earth, Stacey the Real Tooth Fairy discovers a book has been taken that reveals the secret
of how she, as an Earth girl, had a wish to become a fairy and amazingly, her wish came true--
now a certain fairy wannabe is very interested in uncovering that secret.

Library of Congress Control Number: 2009931585
ISBN: 978-0-9841188-1-6
[1.Tooth fairy-Fiction. 2. Fairies-Fiction. 3. Teeth-Fiction 4. Family life-Kindness-Fiction. 5. Magic-Fiction.]
Visit us at www.TheRealToothFairies.com

Love Is Magic

Stacey
The Earth Girl
Becomes a Real Tooth Fairy

As Told by Stacey the Real Tooth Fairy™ to
Rachel E. Frankel

Fairy Portraits by A-M Basom
Stepella & Furry Portraits by Kelly Grupczynski

Book 2

Once upon a day in Real Fairyland, Stacey the Real Tooth Fairy had just finished teaching ballet at the Dancing Dolphins Academy. She left the studio and fluttered down Magic Street to Poof! Potion Shop.

POOF!
Potion Shop

Avalanne was leaving just as Stacey flew in. "Hey, Stacey!" she said. "I'm heading to Surprises Central to get some presents to take to the Earthies. Fly by you later!"

Inside the Potion Shop, Gwendolyn was bottling a new Luscious Lip Dazzle. "How glamorous!" Stacey cooed.

"Thanks!" Gwendolyn said, "It's my new recipe - with extra sparkle!"

Stacey flew to a potion pot and gave one last stir, giggling, "Gwennie, check out my fabberful creation: YOUR-WORDS-R-U! It turns you into the words you speak. So if you say fun words, next stop fun town! But if you say icky words, well . . ."

Stacey poofed the potion into her wand's secret compartment. Gwen asked, "Stacey, is this spell for that rascal Stepella?"

PIG NOSE

UPSIDE DOWN

FLIP

EARS

LAUGH

MONKEY TAIL

PINK STINK

HICCUP

YOUR WORDS R U

Recipe
2 drops of giggles
1 zap of boomerang

YWRU

3

Stacey said, "Yes, and you won't believe Stepella's latest trick. I was in the Fairy Library reading to the tots, when all of a sudden, I saw Stepella tip-toe behind Sir Snoot LaToot, from the Royal Council!

"She followed Sir Snoot and his guard dog, Pepito, as they opened up the SECRET vault. Stepella sneaked behind and fed her Polka-Dotchoo-Gotchoo cookies to Pepito to keep him quiet!"

"Oh, that sneaky rascal!" said Gwendolyn.

"That's not all!" Stacey said as they flew to Surprises Central.

Furry Tales

Official Seal
TOP SECRET

"As Pepito gobbled cookies," Stacey continued, "Stepella snatched a book from the shelf of Secret Books!

Top Secret

"When I called out, 'Stepella, stop!' She waved her flyswatter and yelled, 'Nana-nana boo-boo! I Polka-Dotchoo-Gotchoo!' Then away she ran!"

Gwen sighed, "That Stepella! The Queen gave you a big job to keep her out of trouble!" Stacey agreed, "She just wants to be a fairy, but she goes about it the pranky way."

5

When Stacey flew to Surprises Central, Twinkle, the leader of the Real Tooth Fairies, said, "Hi, Stacey! You have Magic Letters and Kindness Ribbons to deliver tonight. I'll send Yvette Unicorn to help you. And happy news! A girl who lives by your Earthie house lost a tooth!"

TOOTH RECORDS

Stacey cheered, "A visit home!" Happy tears filled her eyes. Twinkle smiled. "I know you love your visits back to see your dad and brother."

Thud! Dublin Elff plopped a sack in Stacey's arms. "For our Earthie boys, Stacey!" he said. "Here are surprises, letters, and Time Travel News about my latest MASK mission — it was very dangerous, of course."

Stacey teased, "Well, I'm sure YOU saved the entire Time Travel Squad, as usual."

GLOW SCORE
FOR Today

UNKIND
5,011

KIND
8,306

*B*rigitte and Triana were gettting ready for their Earth trips, too. Brigitte called out to Stacey, "The Earth Kindess scoreboard is rockin'!" Triana chimed in, "Our Earthie kids are doing a fabberful job of spreading kindness!"

Stacey waved goodbye to her fairy friends and flew to the Earth portal. "Yvette, are we ready?" The unicorn sang, "It's a magical night, twinkles light the sky. With lots of gifts and letters, it's off to Earth we fly!"

At the first house, Stacey magically grew to Earthie size and saw Shannon fast asleep. Stacey had been visiting Shannon since she lost her first tooth two years ago. Shannon loved having her very own Real Tooth Fairy friend!

Stacey read
Shannon's letter:

Dear Stacey Tooth Fairy, It's my 8th birthday! For my birthday wish, will you show me all the kinds of magic you can do?

Love,
Shannon

As soon as Stacey touched Shannon's lost tooth, she saw Shannon's birthday dream inside a glowing Heartwing.

Stacey waved her wand and chanted, *"Abracadagic, love is magic!"* Then she whooshed into Shannon's dream!

9

Yvette Unicorn flew the two friends along a rainbow. Then they stopped on a perfect cloud for bouncing.

*A*fter bounces and giggles, Shannon asked, "Stacey, can you make my hair blue?"

"*C*an you make my brother's stinky feet smell sweet?"

"*C*an you make my cat fly?"

"*C*an you turn that muddy puddle into a swimming pool?"

After granting all Shannon's birthday wishes, Stacey said, "Here's a Magic Letter and a birthday gift just for you! And you did a fantastical kindness today, so here's your award ribbon!"

the umbrella over your table reflects your mood. Ours exploded with smiles and giggles! It was a crazically cool day!

I know your wish will come true, my Earthie friend, as long as you keep believing in you!

Have a fabberful Birthday, my special Earthie friend!

Oodles of Love,
Stacey

Shannon beamed, "My neighbor had surgery, so she was glad when I brought her groceries!" Stacey said, "Way to Glow!"

Shannon hugged Stacey, "This is my BEST birthday ever! You're so magic, you could make anything!" "Well, not quite anything," smiled Stacey. "I could never make the magic that is YOU! I've got to fly for now. Sweet dreams!"

11

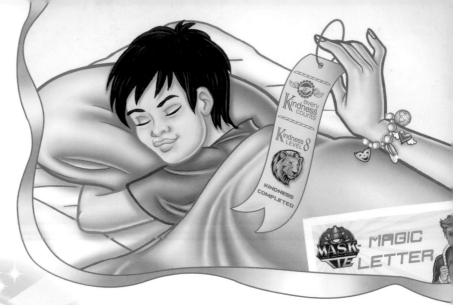

All night, Stacey delivered lost tooth surprises and kindness awards. Jason got a Kindness Ribbon and a Magic Letter from Dublin, his Tooth Elff! On the last stop, Stacey picked up Tamara's lost tooth and saw her dream to be an astronaut in a glowing Heartwing.

In her dream, Tamara showed Stacey her science project. "This is a great step to reach your dream, Tamara," Stacey said. "I'll sprinkle some Glow around you, my awesomous girl!"

Just as she was about to fly off to visit her Earthie house, Stacey's magic wand lit up and shook wildly! "Yvette, what's with my wand? It's tugging on me to go!" Stacey exclaimed. Yvette sang,

"Listen to the wand,
It holds an urgent clue.
Follow it to someone
Who has what belongs to you."

Stacey looked worried, "Do I have to go now? My Earth house is just around the corner!" Yvette answered urgently, "You must go now, go now, go now!"

The wand pulled Stacey outside! "I'll just see my family next trip," she sighed. "Yvette, meet me at Surprises Central later!" Then Stacey zoomed out of sight, bravely following her wand into the night.

13

"Love is the
Magic of a Heart
with Wings"

PART 2

Stacey's Magical Wish

The wand zoomed away flippity fast! As the sun rose, the wand screeched to a halt by a cottage just inside Real Fairyland. The mailbox said: "Stepella, the Fairy Wannabe."

"I should have known this was a Stepella problem!" said Stacey, remembering Yvette Unicorn's song. "I'll peek in Stepella's window to see what she has that belongs to me."

Stacey peered in and gasped, "My Earth Photo Album! THAT'S the book she took from the Secret Vault!" As annoyed as Stacey was with Stepella, she couldn't help smiling to see pictures of when she was an Earthie girl - before she became a Real Tooth Fairy.

Stepella opened the book and cackled, "Ha! This book will show me Stacey-Spacey's secret spell for how to turn into a fairy!"

Stacey's Photos

Meanwhile in the Royal Castle, Sir Snoot brought news to the Queen's guard, Sir Liam. He woke the Queen: "Your Highness, an urgent matter! May I enter with Sir Snoot LaToot?"

Sir Snoot stammered, "Your highness, I'm so, so, so sorry. My guard dog, Pepito, just confessed he ate Stepella's Polka Dotchoo-Gotchoo cookies as she sneak, sneak, SNEAKED a book from the Secret Vault!"

Queen Sirona gasped, "Our Glow Jewels are in that vault! And the secret records . . . of those left behind on Earth." Snoot said, "The oh, oh, ONLY item gone is Stacey's Earth photo album!" Sirona sighed, "That's good news! Please retrieve the book tomorrow." Sir Snoot bowed. "Yes, your highness. Now come naw, naw, NAUGHTY Pepito!"

Back, at the cottage, Stepella opened up the album and crowed, "Oooo, it's baby Stacey sucking her thumb! I never did tha-at!" That was the day Stacey fell off the top of the backyard slide and didn't get hurt, not even a scrape!

A neighbor insisted she saw the two year old Stacey float down to the grass, but no one believed that.

The next picture was Stacey at her mother's ballet school recital. Stepella snorted, "Ha! I can dance better than tha-at!" Stacey smiled, remembering how she used to tell everyone that her mom actually flew when she danced. Of course, no one believed that.

STACEY

Ballet

Then Stepella pointed to the picture of Stacey and her dad making cookies. "Eww, Earthie cookies!" Stepella said. "They don't look half as yummy as my Polka-Dotchoo-Gotchoo cookies!"

*S*tacey smiled as she remembered her mom tucking her into bed. She would gently rub Stacey's hands and feet, while her soft words took Stacey to magical places in her dreams.

Love You Always

Stacey had such happy times with her Earthie family. She still loved to visit her dad and brother, but her mother was in a place where even Real Tooth Fairies couldn't fly.

With Love, Your Fairy Friend Twinkle

Stepella turned to the picture of Stacey's first Real Tooth Fairy surprise. It was a note and a ballet charm bracelet from Twinkle!

"Daddy, just think of it!" Stacey had gushed. "A real fairy was here in MY room!" He hugged her and said, "It sure was a magical night!"

*N*ow, by Stepella's window, Stacey looked at the beautiful bracelet Twinkle gave her years ago. But Twinkle's best gift was showing Stacey that

Love is Magic!

*W*hen young Stacey missed her mom, Twinkle would say, "Close your eyes and feel in your heart all the love you have for each other." Then the two friends would say, "Love is magic!" And something wonderful would happen . . .

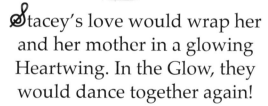

*S*tacey's love would wrap her and her mother in a glowing Heartwing. In the Glow, they would dance together again!

*A*nd Stacey could always have one more hug.

20

The next picture showed Stacey with a trunk full of Magic Letters, Kindness Ribbons, and Dream Tree charms — all from Twinkle, Stacey's bestest friend. Stepella croaked, "Oh, hippo hairballs! I want surprises like THA-AT!"

In a pout, Stepella turned to another photo. In Stacey's 3rd grade class, everyone made a costume of their dream job, and Stacey dressed up as a Real Tooth Fairy! Stepella crowed, "Well, Stacey was a fairy wannabe just like ME! Look at THA-AT!"

My Big Dream

My Job will be a Tooth Fairy

The Job of Being a Tooth Fairy by Stacey

21

Even when Stacey was in high school, Twinkle still flew by to visit. Stacey got goose bumps remembering her 15th birthday. Twinkle had brought Stacey a present, but the Gloom forces tried to trap Twinkle on Earth!

With the portal closed off and Twinkle losing her power, Stacey risked her life to save Twinkle's.

My Future Dreams

be a Real Tooth Fairy

So Queen Sirona granted Stacey one magical wish for her bravery. From the big dream on her Dream Tree, you can see what Stacey wished for!

22

The next photo Stepella saw was Stacey's amazical parade into Real Fairyland when her wish came true! Stacey's dad had agreed she could be a fairy if she'd visit her Earth family as often as possible.

Dreams ♥ Come ♥ True

Stacey

Stepella grumbled, "How did Stacey do tha-at? And why does that Stacey-Smiley-Facey get to be a fairy . . . AND I DON'T!"

"Our world needs
the magic that is
You!"

PART 3

Stepella's Queenie Size Dream

"*Harumph!*"
Stepella fussed as she threw Stacey's book to the floor. "Oooo, I feel a crabby tantrum coming!"
At once, tantrum clouds made the roof bounce and blow its top!

Then she plopped on the floor in a tantrum, kicking her feet. Her bloomers blew up and her cottage jiggled on its springs! Stepella yelled, "AAAGH! I'm feeling CRABBY!"

MINE!
NOT WELCOME
KEEP OUT!

Stacey was jolted out of her memories at the sight of her photo album on the floor beside a tantrumming Stepella. If there was ever a time for her new spell, this was it! She waved her wand and chanted,

"Zippity, zappity, Snappity foo! Make it so
YOUR WORDS R YOU"

Suddenly, Stepella saw her toenails curl and her polka dots droop . . .
then
POOF!

The spell turned Stepella into the crabby words she was saying! She went right on with her tantrum as a crab!

She yelled, "Eek! I'm a crab! I'm REALLY MA-AD now!"

When Stacey flew in, the tantrumming house became still.

Stepella stammered, "Uh, er, oh, Stacey! I didn't TAKE your album! Books in the library are SUPPOSED to be borrowed, right? So I borrowed it. Then it got in the way of my tantrum . . . "

"Stepella," Stacey said, "You know my album from the Secret Vault is not a book to borrow. Why did you take it?"

Stepella plopped to the floor in a crabby heap and stomped her crab claw. "It's NOT fair!" she croaked. "You weren't a fairy and now you are! I wannabe a fairy and I'm NOT! I'm just a Whatsie with no magic!"

Stepella clip-clopped across the floor to get Stacey's book. She looked at Stacey with big, crab eyes and said, "I wanted the book to see HOW you got your magic! You could give me just a little magic! It'd be like one of those kindness-schmindnesses you like to do!"

"Well, Stepella, IF you had a little magic, what would you do with it?"

Stepella cackled, "Why, spells, dearie! My fly swatter would do any magic I wanted! Shazammo! I'd give the Real Tooth Fairies pink and green hair like ME!"

"*Then* wish-a-whoosh! The fairies would wear polka-dot dresses like ME! I'd be queenie-weenie and you'd say, 'Oh, your Step-highness!'"

"*Whoosh*-kazam! Then I'd give everyone hairy legs like ME! And a screechy voice to sing, 'Oh, I wannabe just like Stepell-aah! All the other fairies really smell-aah!'"

29

"Everyone would have tantrums and the castle roof would blow off! Real Fairyland would be a lot more fun with ME in charge!

Of course, Princey Evan would love me instead of Twinkle. And I'd win first place in ALL the fairy contests!"

"Stop right there, my crabby friend," said Stacey, poofing Stepella back to herself. "It's a good thing you don't have magic! And you might win some contests if you actually practiced!"

TIME TRAVEL RESCUE

1st Place Fly Skating

1st Place Singing

Best Kisser

SOCCER CHAMPION

"Practice, schmactice!" squawked Steplla. "No way! Freezee Wizard'll give me some of his magic, so I don't need to practice. He can't resist my Polka-Dotchoo-Gotchoo cookies. You'll see, I'll get magic and one day you'll wake up and be like ME!"

Stacey said, "Gosh Stepella, you want everyone to be YOU! But every girl needs to be her own unique self. You have special gifts, you know!"

"Giftsy-wiftsy! Ho-hum," yawned Stepella. "Take your boring ol' book. No magic secrets in there!"

As Stacey flew away with her photo album, she laughed softly to herself, "Oh, Stepella, if only you could see! The real secret about becoming a fairy WAS right there in the book."

Stepella web-cam

Stepella had no idea that the secret power which saved Twinkle was the magical love in Stacey's heart.

32

Queen Sirona saw the kindness Glow in Earthie Stacey's heart and granted her one wish — and on that magical day, Stacey wished to become a fairy!

But the full tale of that day is another story . . .

And Stacey had no idea that after she left, Stepella found a photo from Stacey's album on the floor. Stepella tucked it in a frame and said, "Ohh, look at them holding hands."

Tears fell from Stepella's eyes. But that's another story, too . . .

The End

Love Is Magic

Twinkle is graduating from Real Fairyversity but she doesn't know what kind of fairy to be. After getting lost on Earth, will she find her true destiny?

Avalanne Fairy cheers her friends on to reach their dreams. But when her friends aren't there for her, will she give up on her own dream?

Triana Fairy has always loved helping Furries in Real Fairyland. But on an Earthie field trip, can she help some Earthie animals in imminent danger?

Stacey says, "Check out the Real Fairyland books to discover the amazical tales of how we became The Real Tooth Fairies!"